Albertine, in Five Times

ALBERTINE
IN FIVE TIMES

a play by Michel Tremblay

**translated by John Van Burek
and Bill Glassco**

Talonbooks   ·   Vancouver   ·   1986

Talon Books
#104-3100 Production Way
Burnaby, British Columbia
Canada V5A 4R4

Typset in Baskerville by Pièce de Résistance, and printed and bound
in Canada by Hignell Printing Ltd.

Fifth Printing: February 2000

Canadian Cataloguing in Publication Data
Tremblay, Michel, 1943-
   [Albertine en cinq temps. English]
   Albertine, in five times

   A play.
   Translation of: Albertine en cinq temps.
   ISBN 0-88922-234-7

   I. Title. II. Title: Albertine en cinq temps. English.
PS8539.R47A513 1986   C842'.54   C86-091460-7
PQ3919.2.T73A513 1986

Albertine, in Five Times was first performed in English by Tarragon Theatre in Toronto, Ontario on April 9, 1985, with the following cast:

Albertine at 30	Susan Coyne
Albertine at 40	Clare Coulter
Albertine at 50	Patricia Hamilton
Albertine at 60	Joy Coghill
Albertine at 70	Doris Petrie
Madeleine	Susan Wright

Directed by Bill Glassco
Set and Costume Design by Astrid Janson
Lighting Design by Harry Frehner

ALBERTINE AT 30 is sitting on the verandah of her mother's house at Duhamel in 1942.

ALBERTINE AT 40 is rocking on the balcony of the house on la rue Fabre in Montreal in 1952.

ALBERTINE AT 50 is leaning on the counter of the restaurant in parc Lafontaine in 1962.

ALBERTINE AT 60 is walking around her bed (in the house on la rue Fabre) in 1972.

ALBERTINE AT 70 has just arrived at a home for the elderly in 1982.

MADELEINE has no age. She acts as confidante to the five Albertines.

ALBERTINE AT 70 enters her room at the home for the elderly. She speaks in short, choppy sentences, almost singing. She has that carefree tone of someone returning from afar. A sprightly little old lady.

ALBERTINE AT 70:

Mind you, they're probably right... I'll be better off... much better. Hard to believe, eh... If someone had told me this a year ago... *She runs her hand over the bed.* The bed's a bit hard... not as bad as the hospital though. The sheets look clean. *She goes to close the door.* I don't know if I'll ever get used to this smell. *She comes back to the bed.* I'll put my television there... so when I sit in my chair I can see fine. Actually, they planned this pretty well. It's small, but they thought about it. It's their job, eh, to figure it out. *She puts her purse on the bed and takes off her coat, which she neatly folds, setting it down beside her purse. She straightens her skirt a bit.* There, I'll be more comfortable. I mean, from now on, this is home. *She sits in her chair.* This was the first thing I tried when I came to look at the place. It's as important as the bed, eh, a good rocker!

> *She rocks for a few moments. ALBERTINE AT 30 steps out onto the verandah of her mother's house at Duhamel. She's a bit plump, but very pretty. She is wearing a light summer dress, circa 1940. She sits in a rocking chair and rocks to the rhythm of ALBERTINE AT 70. The latter notices her and stops rocking, as she lets out a little cry of surprise. They look at each other and smile.*
> *ALBERTINE AT 30 gives a little wave. ALBERTINE AT 70 gives herself a good push and starts rocking again.*

ALBERTINE AT 70:

I've come back from a long way off. Six months ago, I was dead. It's true! They cracked three ribs reviving me. *She laughs.* Crazy, huh? Every time I think of it I can't help laughing. Though it's hardly funny. But what the heck, it's better to laugh than whine about it til you die... a second time... next time for good, I hope! *She laughs.* Not many people can say they've died twice, that's for sure! Mind you, after my second time, I won't be telling anybody anything. I doubt if you come back from the dead more than once.

8

Anyway, when I go back again, I'll be very happy to stay. I've no wish to spend the rest of my days making trips like that, I've never been further than Duhamel in my life!

She looks at ALBERTINE AT 30, who laughs in turn. ALBERTINE AT 40 comes out onto her balcony on la rue Fabre. She's a little fatter than at 30. Her face is harder. She is wearing old clothes, clumsily patched up. At the same time, ALBERTINE AT 50, jovial, singing, and skinny as a rail, plants herself at her counter. She wears a belted dress and her hair is dyed black. She has brought with her a toasted bacon lettuce and tomato sandwich, upon which she chomps away. ALBERTINE AT 70 watches her while she rocks. ALBERTINE AT 30 seems lost in her thoughts.

ALBERTINE AT 70:
When I woke and saw myself with all those tubes and bandages and transfusions... believe me... I felt like going right back where I came from. And when they told me I'd be dragging around for months on end with all that pain...

ALBERTINE AT 60 comes in, stooped, aged, pale. She goes to her bedside table and takes a pill from a plastic container without even checking the label. ALBERTINE AT 70 sighs in exasperation and shifts her chair, turning her back to her. ALBERTINE AT 60 looks at her and shrugs, sits on her bed and rocks from side to side. For a few moments the five ALBERTINES sit silently.

ALBERTINE AT 70:
Mind you, now that it's over, I'm glad to be back.

The other four look at her.

Because things are better. I've got peace. Because here I'll be fine.   *Brief silence.*   Even if I don't like the smell.

*MADELEINE comes out on to the verandah of the house
at Duhamel.*

ALL FIVE ALBERTINES:
Ah, Madeleine!

MADELEINE smiles.

ALBERTINE AT 70:
Hello!

MADELEINE:
Hello!

ALBERTINE AT 70 & 30:
Come and sit down...

*MADELEINE sits beside her sister on the verandah of the
Duhamel house.*

MADELEINE:
Night falls fast here, doesn't it?

ALBERTINE AT 30:
I've never seen anything so beautiful.

*Silence. ALBERTINE AT 70 leans forward a bit to hear
them better.*

Never. It was red, and yellow, the sky, then green... It
never stopped changing.

Silence.

ALBERTINE AT 70:   *moved*
The country...

ALBERTINE AT 30:
> The sun dropped like a rock behind the mountains...
> Just before it disappeared the birds stopped singing.
> Completely. It was like everything, not just me, was
> watching the sun go down. In silence.

ALBERTINE AT 70:
> You talk funny...

> *ALBERTINE AT 30 turns to her.*

ALBERTINE AT 30:
> What?

ALBERTINE AT 70:
> The way you talk, there's something funny...

ALBERTINE AT 30:
> Hmm... It's true, I don't often talk about nature. But if
> you'd seen that, it was so beautiful! When the sun
> disappeared, the birds, the crickets, the frogs started
> their racket again, all of a sudden, as if someone turned
> on a radio.   *Silence.*   In the city...   *Silence.*

ALBERTINE AT 70:
> The country... God, it was beautiful that night!

ALBERTINE AT 30:
> In the city, you never see that...

ALBERTINE AT 70:
> Oh no... In the city, everything's hospital grey...

ALBERTINE AT 50:
> Sometimes when I look out the kitchen window I can
> see that the sky's a yellowy-orange, then pink, then
> lemon-yellow, but the sheds get in the way. I can't see
> what's going on...

ALBERTINE AT 50:
  I can see it.

ALBERTINE AT 30:
  And I don't have time. In the city I never have time for things like that.

ALBERTINE AT 50:
  I take the time!

  ALBERTINE AT 70 laughs.

  It's true! When I finish work sometimes, at night, six o'clock... parc Lafontaine is so beautiful.

ALBERTINE AT 30:
  Not like the country...

ALBERTINE AT 50:
  Of course, not like the country, but so what? In my whole life I saw the country for one week! No point harping on that. No, today, I take what comes. And if it's a big beautiful sunset, I stop and I look at it.

ALBERTINE AT 70:
  You talk funny, too.

ALBERTINE AT 50:
  What do you mean, I talk funny?

ALBERTINE AT 70:
  I don't know... I don't know. It's like you use words I never used...

ALBERTINE AT 50:
  I talk like I talk, that's all...

ALBERTINE AT 30:
  Maybe it's 'cause you don't remember...

ALBERTINE AT 70:
Don't kid yourself... I remember... I remember everything... For the last few months that's all I've had to do, is remember... But it seems to me I never talked nice like that... But don't stop...

ALBERTINE AT 50:
It'll be hard not to stop if you're going to make us talk badly!

ALBERTINE AT 70:
You don't have to talk badly, that's not what I said...

Brief silence. The three ALBERTINES look at one another.

But maybe you're right... I was brought up to think that everything about me was so ugly, I'm amazed to hear I said something beautiful.

Brief silence.

MADELEINE: *to ALBERTINE AT 30*
I brought you some hot milk. It'll help you relax. In his letter Dr. Sanregret says you should have some before bed... It was a bit hot, I've let it cool...

ALBERTINE AT 30:
That's good of you, thanks...

MADELEINE:
But I hope it's not cold... If it's cold, it's no good. Tell me if it's cold, and I'll heat up some more...

ALBERTINE AT 50:
Madeleine!

MADELEINE:
Yes?

13

ALBERTINE AT 50:
  I haven't had milk for ages. Nowadays, it's coke.

MADELEINE:
  You don't need it anymore...

ALBERTINE AT 70:
  I have it sometimes before I go to bed... It reminds me
  of you, Madeleine...

  They look at one another.

  I miss you, you know...

ALBERTINE AT 50:
  Milk plugs you up... Coke delivers!

ALBERTINE AT 30:
  Look, Madeleine, there's still a patch of green. If you
  look at it for a while it turns blue, but when you look
  next to it, out of the corner of your eye, you can see it's
  green.

  *She lifts her head to look at the sky. ALBERTINE AT
  50 and 70 do the same.*

ALBERTINE AT 30, 50 & 70:
  There are so many stars in the sky!

ALBERTINE AT 30:
  And I had to land here, where everything's wrong.

MADELEINE:
  Where did you want to land?

ALBERTINE AT 30:
  Madeleine, do you believe there are other worlds?

ALBERTINE AT 40:
  There'd better be, 'cause this one's no great shakes!

The others look at her.

ALBERTINE AT 40:
Why look at me like that? You think this one's bearable?

ALBERTINE AT 60:
Hell no!

ALBERTINE AT 70:   *sharply*
You be quiet!

ALBERTINE AT 60:
What's the matter?

ALBERTINE AT 70:
I don't want to hear you, that's all...

ALBERTINE AT 50:
Why do you talk to her like that?

ALBERTINE AT 70:
Never mind! Finish your sandwich.

ALBERTINE AT 50:
I've finished my sandwich!

ALBERTINE AT 70:
Then finish your coke.

ALBERTINE AT 50:
I've finished my coke!

ALBERTINE AT 60:
Then finish your squabbling! I'm tired...

ALBERTINE AT 70 turns to her for the first time.

ALBERTINE AT 70:
If you don't shut up...

ALBERTINE AT 60:
> What will you do, eh?

ALBERTINE AT 70:
> I know, I can't do anything. Proof is you're there!

> *ALBERTINE AT 60 blows her nose.*

ALBERTINE AT 60:
> Everybody hates me!

ALBERTINE AT 70:
> No wonder!

ALBERTINE AT 50:
> Stop treating her like that!

ALBERTINE AT 70:
> It's clear you never knew her.

> *She looks at ALBERTINE AT 60 for a few seconds.*

Pathetic!

ALBERTINE AT 40:
> Well, when they announce their first trip to the moon,
> or the sun, I'm going to buy me a one-way ticket, pack
> my little bag, and I'll be happy as a clam.

> *ALBERTINE AT 30 and 50 and MADELEINE
> laugh.*

ALBERTINE AT 50:
> And what in God's name would you do on the moon?

ALBERTINE AT 40:
> I don't know what I'd do, but I sure know what I'd
> leave behind.

ALBERTINE AT 30:
> I wonder if they'll ever make it to the moon...

MADELEINE:
> There's nobody on the moon...

ALBERTINE AT 40:
> Lucky for her!

ALBERTINE AT 70:
> Yeah, they'll make it there, but it won't change much for us...

ALBERTINE AT 60:
> That's hogwash... Do they think we're idiots? I saw them land on the moon, on television... Who're they trying to kid!

ALBERTINE AT 50:
> If they showed it...

ALBERTINE AT 60:
> Don't believe everything they show you!

ALBERTINE AT 40:
> Mind you...

ALBERTINE AT 60:
> Who was there to film them, eh? We saw the two of them, prancing around like gazelles... there was no third guy to make the movie! So how come we could see them?

ALBERTINE AT 30:
> Maybe they had automatic Kodaks...

ALBERTINE AT 60:
> Kodaks? Boy, are you behind the times! They've got these huge buggers now, you should see them... You'd never get them on the moon, not in a hundred years!

ALBERTINE AT 70:
Stop talking nonsense...

ALBERTINE AT 60:
Do you believe them?

ALBERTINE AT 70:
Yes... now I believe them...

ALBERTINE AT 60:
What made you change your mind?

ALBERTINE AT 70:
I've changed a lot... I've read stuff. Now I've got new glasses, I can see, I keep informed. I understand things.

ALBERTINE AT 60 shrugs.

That's right, don't bother to think, shrug your shoulders, that's all you ever do!

ALBERTINE AT 60:
Say what you like, when they give us that crap about trips to the moon and the stars, I switch channels. I'm not kidding, I'd rather watch cartoons and I hate them! There's a bloody limit! And if it's my money they're after, they better not hold their breath! It'll be a cold day in hell before they get a penny from me to build their movie sets and their deep sea costumes to make us believe they're exploring other planets for the good of the human race! Ha! There's enough misery here without looking for it elsewhere! I tell you, when my first pension cheque arrives in the mail, I'll be waiting on the doorstep, and not one of those buggers is going to touch it!

ALBERTINE AT 40:
Mind you, too few people's no better than too many. And it's cold on the moon, I don't like being cold...

18

ALBERTINE AT 50:
> Far as I can tell, you don't like much.

ALBERTINE AT 40:
> Wrong, I don't like anything!

ALBERTINE AT 30:   *lost in her thoughts*
> I could sit here and rock til...   *She smiles*
> *ironically.*   No point in saying til when, eh, that'd be
> dumb.

MADELEINE:
> Stay longer... We're here til September. Uncle Roméo's
> letting us have the house til the kids go back to school.
> Then he'll close it up for the winter.

ALBERTINE AT 30:
> One or two more sunsets won't change my life...
> Besides, when I get home, I won't see them anyway...

ALBERTINE AT 50:
> Get 'em while you can...

ALBERTINE AT 30:
> And I can't spend my life watching the sun go down
> behind a mountain.

ALBERTINE AT 50:
> Why not?

ALBERTINE AT 30:
> If you've got all that free time, good for you... I don't.
> I've got la rue Fabre waiting for me.

ALBERTINE AT 40:   *close to tears*
> La rue Fabre, the kids, the family... Dear God, I'm fed
> up...

ALBERTINE AT 30:
> The kids, the family...

ALBERTINE AT 60:
Who gives a shit about the family!

ALBERTINE AT 70:
The kids... God knows where they are today... Mind you... I do know... I know all too well.

MADELEINE: *after a silence*
You hear that?

ALBERTINE AT 70:
I've survived everyone... and it's not even interesting.

MADELEINE:
Whip-poor-wills. We get them every evening.

ALBERTINE AT 50:
I saw a bird wedding a while ago...

ALBERTINE AT 30:
They sure looked like they were having fun.

ALBERTINE AT 40:
I think they were swallows...

ALBERTINE AT 30:
...but I'm not certain... I don't know about birds. But they were blue... and they gulped their food.

ALBERTINE AT 40:
Is that possible? Swallows in the city? I thought swallows were country birds...

ALBERTINE AT 60:
Who gives a shit about swallows!

ALBERTINE AT 30 takes a deep breath.

ALBERTINE AT 30:
It smells so good it hurts!

20

ALBERTINE AT 70:
Breathe again.

ALBERTINE AT 30 takes another deep breath.

Tell me... tell me what smells like...

ALBERTINE AT 30:
I couldn't say... I don't have words to describe it... it's too good!

MADELEINE gets up, goes toward ALBERTINE AT 70, who looks at her intensely.

MADELEINE:
It smells of freshly cut hay... cow dung too, but just a bit, enough to say it's there... It smells of all the flowers that throw off their perfume before going to bed... It smells of water, muck, the moist earth... It smells green. You know, like parc Lafontaine when they've just cut the grass. Sometimes you're right in the middle of a smell and all of a sudden, just because you move your head a bit it changes... then there's a new smell and you're so surprised you stop breathing so you won't lose it... But it's already gone and another smell has replaced that one... You can sit there on the verandah all evening and count, yes count, the number of different smells that come to visit. *Silence.* It smells of life.

ALBERTINE AT 70 puts her hand over her mouth to keep from crying.

ALBERTINE AT 70:
In the hospital, all you could smell was medication. It was like the other smells were... hidden. Except when someone else in the room was sick, but that's understandable.... Mind you, we were all sick... Me too, at first I guess... I doubt if I smelled too good... but at least I'd apologize. Nobody could say I wasn't polite! The others... Well, a lot of them were pretty confused, eh?... They put me on the floor with the confused, I

21

never did figure out why... I mean, I never lose my head... Anyway... the smells always got covered up sooner or later by the medications or the bleach... 'Cause it was clean, I can't deny that. But here... When I came to visit the first time, I thought... I don't know... that it smelled bland like this 'cause someone had just been sick... But when I came back today it smelled the same. And yet, it seems clean here too. *She seems to have a sudden moment of panic.* What if it always smells like this?

ALBERTINE AT 50 puts down her sandwich.

after a brief silence I guess after I've lived with it for a while, I won't notice it any more.

MADELEINE offers her the cup of milk.

MADELEINE:
Here. Drink your milk. It's going to get cold.

ALBERTINE AT 70 takes the cup and drinks.

ALBERTINE AT 70:
Tastes like the country.

MADELEINE:
You'll sleep better tonight.

ALBERTINE AT 70:
I hope so. You see, it's my first night... naturally I'm a bit nervous...

MADELEINE:
It's real cow's milk, not like in the city. The farmer brings it every morning with cream so thick you can stand a spoon in it.

MADELEINE takes the cup away.

ALBERTINE AT 30:

>Not like the city, you can say that again... In the city, milk like that, they'd call it cream!

>*MADELEINE comes back to ALBERTINE AT 30. Troubled, ALBERTINE AT 70 watches her go.*

ALBERTINE AT 50:

>Here it smells of french fries. Everywhere. All the time. Even my hair and clothes smell of french fries! Before I go out at night though, I put on perfume. I don't know what you'd call a mixture like that, but I like it. I smell good. And strong!

ALBERTINE AT 40:

>Here it smells like a bunch of people who don't belong together... Bickering, jealousy, hypocrisy...

ALBERTINE AT 60:

>Must smell like a tomb in here. I don't dare open the window though, I'll catch my death... I've shut myself up in the house where I was born... hell... in one room of the house... to protect myself from the smell outside. Nothing can touch me now, I've lost my sense of smell.

ALBERTINE AT 70:

>It smells of death in driblets. Did I go through all that to end up here?

>*The others look at her. She blows her nose.*

It'll be better tomorrow.

ALBERTINE AT 60:

>You think so?

ALBERTINE AT 70:

>Yes, I think so!

>*MADELEINE hands the cup of milk to ALBERTINE AT 30 who drinks it slowly.*

ALBERTINE AT 60:

I have no memory of any smells. Not even the pines that made me so dizzy when I arrived at Duhamel. All my life, from then on, when anyone mentions smells, I can see myself standing there on the verandah, filling my lungs with that air! Now... *She looks at MADELEINE.* ...you could spend hours trying to describe that smell to me and I wouldn't remember it.

ALBERTINE AT 30:

Mother's old cup...

ALBERTINE AT 70:

Mother?

MADELEINE:

It's all worn and stained, but not chipped. Sort of like a new antique.

ALBERTINE AT 70:

Who mentioned mother?

ALBERTINE AT 30:

I did.

ALBERTINE AT 70:

I haven't thought of her in ages.

ALBERTINE AT 40:

Lucky you!

MADELEINE:

Strange to think our mother was born right here.

ALBERTINE AT 30:

Yes. Somehow the house is full of her.

ALBERTINE AT 40:

Well I sure think of her! I can't help it, she's on my back all day long!

MADELEINE:

Yet she left here a long time ago. It's funny, we never knew her in this house, but she spoke of it so often, missed it so much, you'd swear she'd forgotten something here, that she'd only just left... Sometimes I open a door and I have the feeling she just walked out of the room... I want to run after her... Crazy, huh?

ALBERTINE AT 30:

She never should have moved to the city... We'd be country folk today, and a lot better off.   *Silence.* Madeleine, I don't want to go back to the city!

ALBERTINE AT 60:

The city... the country... what's the difference!

ALBERTINE AT 40:

I can't stand her any more... and it's mutual.

ALBERTINE AT 30:

I know it's impossible, and my kids need me, even if they're terrified of me, and it's only a week's rest 'cause I'm tired...

ALBERTINE AT 40:

But it's almost over... thank God.

ALBERTINE AT 30:

So tired, Madeleine!

ALBERTINE AT 50:   *to ALBERTINE AT 40*

It's terrible to talk that way about your own mother!

ALBERTINE AT 30:

So tired!

ALBERTINE AT 40:

I know it's terrible. But that's what I think... and it's none of your business.

ALBERTINE AT 50:
Why not? She's my mother too! I know I always fought with her, but I don't remember wishing her dead!

ALBERTINE AT 40:
Well I'm reminding you. When she's gone, we'll be rid of her, you especially.

ALBERTINE AT 50:   *finding her old aggressive spirit*
How can you say such things?

ALBERTINE AT 40:   *in the same tone*
Weren't you relieved when she died?

    Silence.

ALBERTINE AT 50:
I wish I'd never been like you!

ALBERTINE AT 40:
I wish I wasn't going to smell of french fries!

ALBERTINE AT 60:
When she died in her sleep, like a frail little bird... it threw me...   *Silence.*   A hole. Empty.

ALBERTINE AT 50:
Like something missing....

ALBERTINE AT 60:
Yeah, that's right, something was missing... I was going round the house in circles... looking for it... And one day I realized that what I was missing was her insults. She always... fed me... with her insults... and I missed them... 'cause she no longer released what was inside me, like before.

MADELEINE: *to ALBERTINE AT 30*
Forget all that, the city, mother, your problems. Enjoy your vacation. Empty your head.   *Silence.*   Finish your milk.

ALBERTINE AT 30 finishes her milk in one swallow.
ALBERTINE AT 70 makes the gesture of lifting the cup
to her lips.

ALBERTINE AT 70:
You've brought back the cup!

ALBERTINE AT 60:
But I filled the hole. I just took mother's place and
passed the insults on to Thérèse.

ALBERTINE AT 30 sets her cup on the floor, gets up,
and stretches.

ALBERTINE AT 30:
How am I going to sleep with all that racket?

MADELEINE:
I know, they make an awful noise. The crickets are the
worst. They go on all night. But it's funny, that's what
finally puts me to sleep...

ALBERTINE AT 40:
She thinks I'm stupid...

MADELEINE:
Then the frogs wake me up again.

ALBERTINE AT 30 smiles.

ALBERTINE AT 40:
Mother's always thought I'm stupid... You all think I'm
stupid, don't you?

MADELEINE:
Come on, where did you get that?

ALBERTINE AT 40:
I see you, you know... and I hear you! Poor Bartine
this, poor Bartine that, she doesn't understand, but it's
not her fault, she's so stupid...

*MADELEINE moves a little toward ALBERTINE AT
40.*

Well, I may not be too bright, Madeleine, but I've got
eyes and ears.

*MADELEINE has come to sit beside ALBERTINE AT
40.*

MADELEINE:
You know what you're like, Bartine. Some of the things
you say and do make no sense at all.

ALBERTINE AT 40:
Madeleine, I've got a son who's not normal and my
daughter's a wildcat but that doesn't mean they get it
from me! My husband was also there when I made
those kids! Sure, none of you talk about him, he
disappeared long ago, he was a war hero who did us
proud, how could he be anything but perfect! But you
all forget one thing: he was a moron! He was the idiot,
Madeleine, not me. Who else but an idiot would go and
get himself killed for nothing on the other side of the
ocean? I bet you anything he ran right out in front of
them playing the hot shot, and there's no way he died a
hero, he died a buffoon. A buffoon! He was a buffoon,
Madeleine! But it's me who's here, me, so it's easy to
judge me!

MADELEINE:
I never said you were crazy or wild or that your kids
get it from you...

ALBERTINE AT 40:
Baloney! You all decided long ago I wasn't intelligent.
Just because I don't understand things your way doesn't
mean I'm not intelligent. There's more than one kind of
intelligence, you know. The rest of you... you're
intelligent with your heads but you refuse to accept that
someone can be... I don't know how to say it,

28

Madeleine... With me it's not my head that works,
it's... it's my instincts, I guess. I know I do things
without thinking, but I'm not always wrong, am I? Ever
since I was a kid people give me these funny looks
whenever I open my mouth because I say what I
think... You condemn what I say, but you don't hear
yourselves! You ought to use your heads less and your
hearts more. And you never listen to me! The minute I
open my mouth I get this look of contempt that's so
insulting! You're so convinced I'm a jerk you don't even
listen to me any more.

MADELEINE:
Why do you say that... What am I doing now?

ALBERTINE AT 40:
Sometimes you enrage me, Madeleine, with your
superior airs!

MADELEINE:
Oh, don't start that again...

ALBERTINE AT 40:
Sure, I know, I'm supposed to put up with it and say
nothing, but the minute I speak everyone shits on me.

MADELEINE:
What do you expect, you're impossible! We can't say a
word to you, you start swinging, you don't think!

ALBERTINE AT 40:
There you go, just like mother!

MADELEINE:
I don't know what mother says...

ALBERTINE AT 40:
Madeleine, that's a lie!

Silence.

29

You see, you can't answer...

MADELEINE:
How can you answer someone as stubborn as you!

ALBERTINE AT 70:
Poor Madeleine... I put you through the wringer, didn't I... but I wonder if you knew how much I loved you...

MADELEINE looks at her.

MADELEINE:
No. We never knew if you loved us or hated us... so often you said you hated us. To each of us in turn, or all of us together... At times that's all we got from you, we could feel it, almost touch it.

ALBERTINE AT 40:
You don't know what it's like, to feel alone in a house full of people! Nobody listens to me because I'm always screaming and I'm always screaming because nobody listens! I don't let up from morning to night. By noon I'm exhausted. I run after Marcel to protect him, and I run after Thérèse to stop her from getting into worse trouble than the day before. And I yell louder at mother than she yells at me! I'm fed up, Madeleine, fed up with always being in a rage! I'm smart enough to see your contempt for me, but not clever enough to shut you up!

MADELEINE:
Don't shout, Bartine! Try to speak in a softer voice...

ALBERTINE AT 40:
I can't... My heart is bursting with things that are so ugly, if you only knew...

Silence.

ALBERTINE AT 50:
　　It will pass...

ALBERTINE AT 60:
　　Yeah, but it'll come back...

ALBERTINE AT 40:
　　And when you come strutting in here with your whiz
　　kids and your perfect husband...

　　　MADELEINE puts her hand on her sister's arm.

MADELEINE:
　　I don't "strut" in here, and you know it...

ALBERTINE AT 40:
　　Come off it! If you can find fault with everything I say
　　and do, I can do likewise. You come here to shove your
　　happiness under my nose, make sure I'll get a good
　　sniff! Your oldest is always top of the class, Thérèse is a
　　waitress in some dive. Your youngest is funny as a
　　monkey; meanwhile Marcel retreats more and more into
　　himself.

　　　MADELEINE gets up.

　　Don't run away!

MADELEINE:
　　Trying to talk to you when you're like this is hopeless.
　　You won't listen...

ALBERTINE AT 40:
　　Seems we all have that problem... When it's my turn to
　　speak, it's never interesting, is it?

ALBERTINE AT 50:
　　I'm getting sick of you...

31

ALBERTINE AT 40:
>That's right, take their side too!

ALBERTINE AT 50:
>I'm not, but you're talking in circles.

ALBERTINE AT 40:
>And I suppose they're not?

MADELEINE:
>It's impossible to talk to you. You can't control your temper! The number of times I've sat with you, trying to have a discussion... Within five minutes all hell breaks loose, we're ready to kill each other... every time!

ALBERTINE AT 70:
>If you'd taken another tone with me I might have been capable of discussion.

>*MADELEINE looks at her.*

MADELEINE:
>You agree with her?

ALBERTINE AT 70:
>You bet!

ALBERTINE AT 40:   *suddenly*
>The first time someone's understood me!

ALBERTINE AT 70:
>'Cause you went about it all wrong...   *to*
>*MADELEINE*   You know what I wanted you to do, Madeleine? No, not what I wanted, I don't think I wanted it... but what you should have done.

MADELEINE:
>What?

ALBERTINE AT 70:
It wasn't discussion I wanted... we had that day in and
day out... no, I needed you to put your arms around
me, to hold me...

ALBERTINE AT 50:   *softly*
I haven't been touched by anyone for so long.

ALBERTINE AT 40:
That's not true. That's not what I needed.

ALBERTINE AT 50:
Oh yes it is!

ALBERTINE AT 40:
Are you judging me too? Is that it? You know better
than me what I need?

ALBERTINE AT 70:
We're not judging you...

ALBERTINE AT 50:
...we remember.

ALBERTINE AT 40:   *to MADELEINE*
Keep away from me!

   MADELEINE approaches her and takes her in her arms.

MADELEINE:
I didn't know, Bartine...

ALBERTINE AT 40:
Don't touch me! Leave me alone!

   They remain frozen for moment. Nothing moves on the
   stage. ALBERTINE AT 40 has kept her eyes wide open,
   as if terrorized.

MADELEINE: *very gently*
Relax...

ALBERTINE AT 40:
I can't.

MADELEINE:
I hug my own kids all the time, I should have realized.
But with a sister who's always in a rage, it's not so
easy... Relax... let yourself go... Think... think of
Duhamel, ten years ago... Remember how beautiful it
was?

ALBERTINE AT 40:
You won't get me with sentiment! My rage is too great.

ALBERTINE AT 60:
At times, I sort of remember... physical contact. I mean
my head remembers. And it's so revolting, I thank my
stars I don't know a soul any more.

ALBERTINE AT 30:
Madeleine?

MADELEINE:
Yes?

ALBERTINE AT 30:
What did Dr. Sanregret say in his letter?

MADELEINE:
Well, he said you should rest 'cause you've had a bad
shock.

ALBERTINE AT 40 pushes her away.

ALBERTINE AT 40:
If I took a rest every time I had a bad shock, I'd have
spent my life in the sanatorium!

34

ALBERTINE AT 30:
Did he tell you everything? The whole story?

ALBERTINE AT 40:
Are you kidding, the whole world knows my problems.
That's all they ever talk about.

MADELEINE:
I don't know what happened, Bartine. There's no
electricity here... no telephone...

ALBERTINE AT 40:
Goddamned liar! I've got you now! You get a letter
from Dr. Sanregret who sends you this letter to tell you
I need a rest 'cause I've had a bad shock, and he
doesn't even tell you what it was! You take me for an
idiot?

ALBERTINE AT 30:
Did he tell you I almost killed Thérèse?

The others look at her.

MADELEINE:
No... He says you gave her a beating, but...

ALBERTINE AT 40:
Don't believe her!

ALBERTINE AT 30:
I want to believe her. I want to get it off my chest!

ALBERTINE AT 40:
Why bother? She'll only despise you more...

ALBERTINE AT 30:
Madeleine, I almost killed Thérèse.

ALBERTINE AT 40:
That's right, confess! Trust her. It's your funeral. You'll
have the whole family laughing behind your back.

35

MADELEINE: *to ALBERTINE AT 30*
Aren't you exaggerating...

ALBERTINE AT 30:
If Gabriel hadn't arrived, I think I would have killed
her.

ALBERTINE AT 40:   *to herself*
Maybe you should have. I wouldn't be screaming on my
balcony right now, like some nut in a strait jacket!

ALBERTINE AT 30:
I have this huge force inside me, Madeleine. I have a
power in me, that scares me.   *Silence.*   To
destroy.   *Silence.*   I didn't ask for it. It's there. If
I hadn't been so miserable, I might have forgotten it or
conquered it, but there are time... times when I feel...
this rage, yes, rage, Madeleine. I'm crazy with
rage.   *Silence. She lifts her arm a bit.*   Look... the
size of that sky. That whole sky couldn't contain my
rage.   *Silence.*   If I could explode, Madeleine...
But I'll never explode... Not after what I did to
Thérèse. I'm too scared.

MADELEINE:
You want to tell me about it?... It might help.

ALBERTINE AT 40:
You're dying to know, aren't you? There's no phone,
but there is one in the village! And it won't be long
before mother knows everything!

MADELEINE:
Stop interrupting all the time. If I'm such a liar don't
talk to me. Don't phone me ten times a day to
complain; don't come bawling to our place three times a
week... Decide one way or the other, Bartine. Either
speak your mind, or never speak to me again!
Silence.   Your accusations are ridiculous!   *Silence.*
You're not so important that we spend our time spying
on you...

ALBERTINE AT 40:
Then leave me alone! Forget about me. Pretend I don't exist!

MADELEINE:
Sure, and in two days you'll say we abandoned you!

ALBERTINE AT 40:
Ah, go to hell, the lot of you!

MADELEINE moves away from ALBERTINE AT 40 and sits on the edge of the verandah at Duhamel.

MADELEINE:
You don't have to tell me...

ALBERTINE AT 70:
It's so difficult!

ALBERTINE AT 30:
You'd think we were alone in the world, just the two of us...

ALBERTINE AT 70:
It's so dark all of a sudden...

ALBERTINE AT 60:
Makes you want to whisper...

ALBERTINE AT 40:
No, makes you want to destroy everything!

ALBERTINE AT 50:
The moon's not up yet. The full August moon is always late.

ALBERTINE AT 30:
From down there on the road, the house must look like a lantern. I wonder if someone going by could see us here... From that distance they probably couldn't tell I'm a criminal, eh? *She closes her eyes.*

ALBERTINE AT 40:
> They don't need binoculars to see that.

ALBERTINE AT 30:
> If you only knew, Madeleine, it hurts so
> much.   *Silence. She opens her eyes. She sighs.*   One
> week off. A week's rest. Then it starts all over again...

MADELEINE:
> It's our role, Bartine....

> *ALBERTINE AT 30 suddenly turns to MADELEINE.*

ALBERTINE AT 30:
> Our role! It's not our role. It's our lot!

> *She sits in the rocker again.*

ALBERTINE AT 70:
> Shhh... not so loud. Think before you speak.

ALBERTINE AT 30:
> I know, your lot's better than mine, but... don't you
> feel... don't you feel you're in a hole, Madeleine, a
> tunnel, a cage?

ALBERTINE AT 60:
> A cage... Ah, yes... a cage.

MADELEINE:
> I don't know what you mean, Bartine...

ALBERTINE AT 60:
> In a cage! You know what that is, a cage!

> *MADELEINE turns to her.*

With bars! Bars, Madeleine, that keep you from getting
out! Because it's you who's in the cage!

ALBERTINE AT 70:
   You asked for it!

ALBERTINE AT 60:
   That's not true!

ALBERTINE AT 70:
   Look at yourself! A cage is all you deserve!

ALBERTINE AT 30:
   In ten, twenty years, we'll still be here, in our cage with
   bars. And when we're old, when they don't need us any
   more, they'll put us in cages for old women. And we'll
   go crazy with boredom!

ALBERTINE AT 70:
   No, that's not true...

MADELEINE:
   What makes you think this way all of a sudden,
   Bartine?

ALBERTINE AT 70:   *a little stronger*
   Not true!

ALBERTINE AT 30:
   I don't know.   *Silence.*   I don't know. It's not like
   me to rebel.

ALBERTINE AT 60:
   Rebel?

ALBERTINE AT 70:
   If I'm here, it's not because they don't need me any
   more... it's because I'm alone.

ALBERTINE AT 30:
   I guess what's happened has really thrown me...

ALBERTINE AT 70:
All alone. Like a dog!

ALBERTINE AT 60: *ironically*
To rebel?

ALBERTINE AT 40: *to ALBERTINE AT 30*
Talk about your rage.

ALBERTINE AT 30:
What?

ALBERTINE AT 40:
Talk about your rage!

ALBERTINE AT 60:
It never does any good to rebel...

ALBERTINE AT 70:
No, I mustn't give in to despair... Help me!

> *ALBERTINE AT 50 goes over to ALBERTINE AT 70. She gently takes her hand.*

Thank you.

ALBERTINE AT 60:
It's childish to rebel. The punishment is always too great.

ALBERTINE AT 30:
It's my rage, Madeleine... my rage wants to strike out...

ALBERTINE AT 60:
And when the rage comes back...

ALBERTINE AT 30:
But I don't know how, or where, or at whom!

ALBERTINE AT 60:
Words... can't describe... the impotence of rage.

ALBERTINE AT 50: *to ALBERTINE AT 70*
You're not alone. Think of us. We're all here, with
you...

ALBERTINE AT 70:
Not all of you are a consolation...

ALBERTINE AT 50:
Don't just think of our bad points... There are times...
times when you were okay... Look at Thérèse and
Marcel... We know what became of them, and it's easy
to dwell on that... but how about when they were little,
eh? Did you ever see two such adorable babies? You
remember?

ALBERTINE AT 70:
Yes, I remember, but it's no comfort...

ALBERTINE AT 50:
Try... for my sake.

ALBERTINE AT 70:
Mind you, they were lovely babies. When Thérèse was
small, people would stop me on the street to tell me how
lovely she was...

ALBERTINE AT 50:
And Marcel...

ALBERTINE AT 70:
Marcel had too much imagination... he frightened me,
even when he was little...

ALBERTINE AT 50:
But think of all the cuddles... how he'd laugh when he
was happy...

ALBERTINE AT 70:
>None of that's clear for me now... What became of
>them is too painful... I can't recall the good moments...
>I'm sorry.

ALBERTINE AT 60:
>Impotence...

ALBERTINE AT 50:
>If it's not clear... make it up. If the past is too painful,
>invent a new one... Do what I did, forget! At least try.
>You'll see, it's not so hard. When a bad memory tries to
>get me, I shake it off... If I'm in the house, I get out...
>If I'm at work, I sing... I turn my back on it, leave it
>behind.

ALBERTINE AT 70:
>Where can I go? Out in the hall? They'd catch up with
>me in no time. You see, I can't go anywhere, I can't
>rebel.

ALBERTINE AT 60:
>Exactly. That's why I'm resigned to it. You can never
>get away, never!

ALBERTINE AT 70:
>You're not resigned to anything. You've just let go.
>You've given up... life. It's not the same.

ALBERTINE AT 50:
>That's right... so don't copy her.

ALBERTINE AT 60:
>You talk about me like I'm dead.

>*ALBERTINE AT 70 looks at her, then turns away.*

ALBERTINE AT 70:   *to ALBERTINE AT 50, tapping her
on the hand*
>I'll be okay...

ALBERTINE AT 50 slowly leaves her.

ALBERTINE AT 40:
It's like a ball of fire, Madeleine...

ALBERTINE AT 30:
Yes... A ball of fire in my chest...

ALBERTINE AT 40:
...that never stops burning.

ALBERTINE AT 30:
Even if I scream, if I hit people, it's still there... even after I've calmed down...

ALBERTINE AT 40:
Sometimes it hurts so much I can't do a thing... I have to lie down on the bed... but then it gets worse....

ALBERTINE AT 30:
To lie on your bed in a rage, Madeleine... is horrible!

MADELEINE:
But what gets you so enraged?

ALBERTINE AT 40:
Everything!

ALBERTINE AT 30:
That's right, I take everything badly... Even the good times... the few I get. When something goes right for me I don't trust it... I think there's something dreadful I can't see, and it's going to pounce on me.

MADELEINE:
Why not enjoy the good times while they're happening...

ALBERTINE AT 30:
I can't.

ALBERTINE AT 50:
That's not true...

ALBERTINE AT 40:
They're always followed by something hideous.
to ALBERTINE AT 50   You'll see!

MADELEINE:
But that happens to everyone. We're all the same. You
don't have a monopoly on suffering.

ALBERTINE AT 40:
Will you stop telling me that! I know I don't have a
monopoly on suffering. But how come what happens to
me is always worse than what happens to others?

MADELEINE:
Because you make it worse. Instead of looking for a
solution, you rush headlong into tragedy and disaster.

ALBERTINE AT 30:
Easy for you to say, nothing ever happens to you.

MADELEINE:
You think that because I don't complain, Bartine. I keep
my troubles to myself. Deal with them myself.

ALBERTINE AT 60:
I do that now too, Madeleine... I took your advice...
I stay quiet in my room, I don't bother a soul...

*She opens a small bottle of pills and takes one with a glass
of water.*

And for the first time, I've got peace.

ALBERTINE AT 50:
You've got a short memory.

44

ALBERTINE AT 60:
> What? I don't know what you mean.

ALBERTINE AT 50:
> I've stopped complaining too... But I don't take pills...

ALBERTINE AT 60:
> That won't last...

ALBERTINE AT 50:
> Why shouldn't it?

ALBERTINE AT 60:
> Because you're play-acting. You're going through a phase where you play at being happy and positive.

ALBERTINE AT 70:
> Oh, shut up!

ALBERTINE AT 60:
> You're no different! You've convinced yourself you'll be happy in your stinky little room, but the real you knows better.

ALBERTINE AT 70:
> At least I'm glad to be alive...

ALBERTINE AT 50:
> So am I... glad to be alive...

ALBERTINE AT 60:
> I don't believe you.

ALBERTINE AT 30:
> I'm young, I'm strong, I could do so much if it weren't for this rage, gnawing at me...

ALBERTINE AT 40:
> Sometimes I think it's all that keeps me alive...

ALBERTINE AT 30:
It's true...

ALBERTINE AT 60:
You'll get over that, too... Rage... Rebellion never solved a thing.

ALBERTINE AT 30:
I'll tell you why I'm here this week, Madeleine, you'll understand... You'll understand what I mean by this rage. *Silence. The other ALBERTINES and MADELEINE listen carefully.* My child, my own daughter, my Thérèse, who I fight with all the time because we're so alike... though I try to bring her up as best I can... It's true, you know, I do the best I can... I don't know much, but what I do know I try to pass on to my kids... though they never listen. Another thing that enrages me... Anyway... my Thérèse who I always thought was so innocent, with her dolls and those girlfriends she leads around by the nose... Believe it or not, she was seeing a man. A man, Madeleine, not some brat her own age who'd be happy to kiss her with her mouth closed, but a grown man!

MADELEINE:
Are you sure? She's only eleven!

ALBERTINE AT 30:
When I found out I went berserk... I mean, you'd have done the same. I know, don't say it, your daughter would never do that...

MADELEINE:
But who is he? Did you ever see them together?

ALBERTINE AT 30:
Of course not, for God's sake, I'd have murdered him long ago! She wasn't seeing him... actually going out with him, no, that's not what I mean... *Silence.*

46

ALBERTINE AT 70:
Go on... it'll do you good.

ALBERTINE AT 30:
I know it will, but I can't.   *She takes two or three deep
breaths.*   Did you ever want to destroy everything
around you? Did you ever feel you had the strength to
destroy everything?   *She searches for the
words.*   Men... men... men... They're the ones,
Madeleine. They're the ones. Not us.

> *MADELEINE approaches her sister and takes her in her
> arms. ALBERTINE AT 30 withdraws from this timid
> hug.*

Eleven years old, Madeleine, and he was chasing her
like she was a woman! Following her everywhere. And
she let him do what he liked, without a word. She
knew, and she didn't say a word!

ALBERTINE AT 40:
She liked it.

ALBERTINE AT 30:
She liked it, Madeleine, she told me herself. And that's
why I beat her.

ALBERTINE AT 40:
And she still likes it... after all that's happened... that's
what's killing me.

ALBERTINE AT 50:
Why drag it all up again? Leave it be, for God's sake!

ALBERTINE AT 30:
Naturally I found out by accident. I was lying on the
sofa the other day, in the middle of the afternoon... I
could feel a storm brewing... Mother'd been in a rotten
mood all day, the kids were driving me nuts... Thérèse
came to sit on the front balcony with her friend
Pierrette.   *Silence.*

ALBERTINE AT 40:
They talked about it like it was an everyday thing...

ALL FIVE ALBERTINES: *in alternation*
Pierrette asked Thérèse if she'd seen her "gent" lately
and she said he disappeared the beginning of June. I
assumed it was some neighbourhood kid, and I figured:
"Here we go, boy problems. Already." Then I realized
it wasn't that at all. They were talking about him like
he was an actor, for God's sake. Comparing him to
those movie stars in the magazines... They even said he
was better looking! I lay there, horrified... They had no
idea... of the danger... the danger of men, Madeleine...

ALBERTINE AT 30:
And when Thérèse started talking about the last time
she saw him, how he got down on his knees in front of
her right on the street and put his head on... her belly,
I got up, not knowing what I was doing and went out
on the balcony...

ALL FIVE ALBERTINES: *in alternation*
...and I started to hit her, Madeleine.

ALBERTINE AT 30:
I didn't know where I was hitting, I just hit her as hard
as I could. Thérèse was screaming, Pierrette was crying,
the neighbours coming out of their houses... and I
didn't stop... I couldn't. It wasn't just Thérèse I was
hitting, it was... my whole life... I couldn't find the
words to explain the danger, so I just hit!   *She turns
toward her sister.*   I never told Thérèse much about
men 'cause the words would have been
filthy.   *Silence.*   If Gabriel hadn't come out and
separated us, I would have killed her.

*MADELEINE puts her hand on her sister's shoulder who
throws herself into her arms.*

48

I didn't cry, Madeleine. Not once. And I still
can't. *Silence.*   Rage.

ALBERTINE AT 40:
> Thérèse was never worth tears.

ALBERTINE AT 70:
> How can you say that? She's your child!

ALBERTINE AT 40:
> And yours. Do you even remember her? Shed tears for
> her?

> *Silence.*

ALBERTINE AT 70:
> I have my regrets.

ALBERTINE AT 40:
> But no tears.

> *Silence.*

ALBERTINE AT 70:
> I never knew how to cry.

> *ALBERTINE AT 30 and MADELEINE have sat
> down on the steps.*

ALBERTINE AT 30:
> Is that what the doctor said in his letter?

MADELEINE:
> No. He said you gave Thérèse a beating. Since neither
> of you told him why, he didn't know.

ALBERTINE AT 30:
> I guess he thinks I'm crazier than ever.

MADELEINE:
> No one thinks you're crazy.

ALBERTINE AT 30:
> But I am, you know. When your child's in danger and
> you beat her instead of explaining it to her, isn't that
> crazy?

ALBERTINE AT 70:
> No, it's not crazy. It's ignorance.

> *MADELEINE lowers her eyes.*

> *to MADELEINE*   Why don't you tell her?

MADELEINE:
> What...

ALBERTINE AT 70:
> That it's ignorance...

MADELEINE:
> You don't just tell your sister she's ignorant.

ALBERTINE AT 70:
> If it can help her...

MADELEINE:
> And what if it doesn't?

ALBERTINE AT 70:
> Well I'll tell you, you're ignorant, even if you are my
> sister.

MADELEINE:
> I see you haven't changed as much as I thought.

ALBERTINE AT 70:
> Don't misunderstand. If you tell her she's not crazy,
> she'll believe you; if you tell her it's ignorance, and
> ignorance can be overcome, that may encourage her... I
> don't know... to find out, ask questions...

ALBERTINE AT 30:
Never mind... don't bother. It's nice that you care, but whether I'm stupid or crazy won't change a thing. I know I'm not like the others...

ALBERTINE AT 70: *gently*
But... the others are no smarter.

ALBERTINE AT 40:
That's why I yell at them, too!

ALBERTINE AT 70:
Excuse me, I'm not talking to you... *to* *ALBERTINE AT 30* We all depend on you... Try... to talk to Thérèse... to understand Marcel. Once they're gone, it will be too late...

ALBERTINE AT 50:
Not for me...

ALBERTINE AT 30:
I try sometimes... I really do. But we're the same, all three of us... pigheaded... and... we can't talk to one another. *to ALBERTINE AT 70* Don't judge me. You've forgotten how hard it is.

ALBERTINE AT 70:
Mind you... there's no point in asking people to change... When you're young you think you're right... when you get older you realize you were wrong... what's the point of it all? We should have the right to a second life... but we're so badly made... I doubt we'd do any better.

ALBERTINE AT 30: *to MADELEINE*
Did the doctor ask you to try and get me to talk?

MADELEINE:
No.

Silence.

ALBERTINE AT 30:
What am I going to, Madeleine?

MADELEINE:
Do you know who the guy is?

ALBERTINE AT 30:
I think he works at parc Lafontaine. They're the worst. They're supposed to keep an eye on our kids, and they spend their time ogling them... I'll sic the cops on him when I get home...

ALBERTINE AT 40:
No, you won't sic the cops on him... All you'll do is punish Thérèse and try to forget. And when you do find him, it'll be too late.

ALBERTINE AT 30:
But that's not what I meant... What do I do for the rest of my life? If I beat my kids just 'cause I can't talk to them, does that mean they'll lock me up? Even when I'm right?

ALBERTINE AT 60:
No, they won't do that... You'll lock them up...

ALBERTINE AT 30:
Me, lock up my kids? What do you mean?

ALBERTINE AT 50:
Never mind, I know what she's up to...

ALBERTINE AT 60:
You're scared, huh?

ALBERTINE AT 50:
Yes. I'm scared of your version.

ALBERTINE AT 60:
 There's more than one?

ALBERTINE AT 50:
 Okay, if we really have to talk about it, let me go first...
 then we'll see.

ALBERTINE AT 60:
 Don't listen to her. She'll embellish it, she'll make
 herself look good.

ALBERTINE AT 50:
 I'll tell what happened, the way it happened.

 Silence.

ALBERTINE AT 70:
 Be careful... this is a delicate matter...

ALBERTINE AT 50:
 I know, but I'm not ashamed of it.

ALBERTINE AT 70:
 Fine. Go ahead...

ALBERTINE AT 50:
 One day I discovered something really important. I did
 it myself, too, even if I'm no genius... I was thinking
 about my kids and my family who never listened to me,
 never gave me the time of time, never asked my opinion
 and who treated me like I didn't exist. And I discovered
 that to make yourself heard in this life, you have to
 disobey. If you really want something, you *disobey*.
 Otherwise you get crushed. I always listened to others,
 took their advice, did what they wanted, you,
 Madeleine, our two brothers, mother... but at the age of
 fifty I disobeyed, and I'm not sorry.

ALBERTINE AT 60:
 You will be...

ALBERTINE AT 50:
It was hard at first... I'd always depended totally on others. No kidding, if someone didn't tell me what to do, I asked. I begged! I spent my life begging. There I was, stuck in this houseful of people, and I couldn't budge until someone said it was okay. And all that did was feed my rage... I was always about to explode. But at the age of fifty I thought, don't ask me any more. Disobey. Try it, just once. Find out if it works. But I had this huge weight holding me back... Marcel. Thérèse had disappeared long ago. I never heard from her except when they found her drunk in some alley, or she'd phone me from headquarters 'cause they'd just picked her up... How many times I had to scrape together the twenty-five bucks, then take the Saint-Denis bus... I tell this like it was nothing, but... we get numbed by the pain, I guess... So Marcel was all I had left, twenty-five years old, barely responsible, a child for life, who I was still protecing and would go on protecting until one of us dropped because I never could understand him... He withdrew more and more, drifted away from me, yet still demanding I be there... I watched him... Yes, I watched him go mad... I'm sorry, this isn't easy...

ALBERTINE AT 60:
Costs a lot to disobey, huh?

ALBERTINE AT 70:   to *ALBERTINE AT 60*
Will you please shut up!

ALBERTINE AT 50:   to *MADELEINE*
I didn't stick to my role, Madeleine, I disobeyed. I know what you all thought, but you were wrong. If I hadn't done it, if I were still the prisoner of a madman, a madman who had me in the palm of his hand, who was growing more and more dangerous... that's not a role for anyone. I broke the mould, I stopped being mother hen.   *Silence.*   I told Thérèse I'd have nothing more to do with her... and I had Marcel put away, far from here...

54

MADELEINE turns away.

It hurt, but you want to know the truth? I've never been happier in my life, and neither have they. They're with their own kind, and so am I.

ALBERTINE AT 40:
You should have done it sooner... If I had the guts... but I'm scared what people would think.
ironically   We play our roles to the bitter end, don't we? So they always told us. You brought a crazy kid into the world, it's your fault, pay!

ALBERTINE AT 50:
When it was over, and I'd done it, and I found myself alone, it was incredible. A feeling I'd never known. My days were mine, no one to worry about... I bought new clothes, not expensive, but nice, and I went out to find a job. Do you realize what that means? A job. Freedom!

ALBERTINE AT 70:
My first job. My only job. Le parc Lafontaine.

ALBERTINE AT 50:
The only park I've ever known, the only bit of green, and it's mine. I work in the restaurant at parc Lafontaine, right in the very heart where everyone goes... and they say I make the best bacon, lettuce and tomato sandwich with mayo in the world! People come here especially for my BLT's. They come to me 'cause I'm the best! And what's more, I get paid! The customers and the other employees love me, and they treat me like a queen because I feed them like they used to get fed at home.

ALBERTINE AT 60:
You wait on people like you always did.

ALBERTINE AT 50:

At least I'm not down on all fours cleaning up Marcel's mess or getting ulcers 'cause Thérèse has pulled another stunt! I come here singing in the morning, I sing while I work, and I go home singing at night. I watch the sun set in summer and the kids skating in winter. I earn my living, do you understand? I live as I please without family on my back, without kids, without men! Oh yes, no men. By choice. And I'm happy. I held myself back too long, Madeleine. I had to disobey!

MADELEINE:

You hate them that much?

ALBERTINE AT 30:

My kids?

ALBERTINE AT 50:

I love my kids more than my life, Madeleine. But they're better off away from me, and I'm better off away from them.

MADELEINE:

I'm not talking to you...   *to ALBERTINE AT 30*   I don't mean your kids...

ALBERTINE AT 50:

You've had enough of me?

MADELEINE:

I'm talking about men.

ALBERTINE AT 30 stiffens. She doesn't answer.

ALBERTINE AT 60:

Who wants to listen to a heartless cow?

ALBERTINE AT 70:

Why heartless?

ALBERTINE AT 60:
> To abandon her kids....

ALBERTINE AT 40:
> I understand you.

ALBERTINE AT 70:
> So do I...I think.

MADELEINE:
> Because you knew one who was a bastard doesn't mean
> they're all like that.

> *Silence. ALBERTINE AT 50 laughs wickedly.*

ALBERTINE AT 50:
> The gospel according to Madeleine! I know it by heart.

MADELEINE:
> Soon, in about half an hour...we're going to see two
> lights in the distance...two narrow beams that will light
> up the pines on either side of the highway...The car will
> turn left up the driveway...Alex will be home...with
> treats for me and the kids...corn on the cob, though it's
> not in season yet, or candies, or a nice plump chicken
> he's got in exchange for God knows what...You know
> salesmen, all kinds of tricks up their sleeves...He'll give
> me a little wave as he gets out of the car. I'll go down
> the steps to meet him...It's exciting, a kiss in the dark.
> His eyes will be gentle when he looks at me, even
> though he can't see me, and I can't see him either.

ALBERTINE AT 50:
> Her favourite role...always the same...

ALBERTINE AT 70:
> You were so naive, Madeleine...

MADELEINE:
> Alex is a good man, Bartine....

ALBERTINE AT 30:
Well, that's fine for you...but he's the only one you've ever known.

MADELEINE:
I prefer to think well of them.

ALBERTINE AT 30:
Well, I don't. Wait til your daughter comes to you with a problem like Thérèse's...

MADELEINE:
That's not likely. My daughter and I talk...

ALBERTINE AT 40:
Talk to Thérèse, see how much fun that is! You can't, I've been telling you for ten years. She's not a little girl any more, she's got real problems!

MADELEINE:
You don't know how to deal with her...

ALBERTINE AT 40:
I've tried everything under the sun! All she does is shit on me, then goes right back to her pimps and whores.

ALBERTINE AT 30:
I don't want her to end up like me, but I don't want her to rebel so much she ruins her life.

ALBERTINE AT 40:
Well, that's what she's done. And it's no fun to watch.

ALBERTINE AT 30:
I wish I knew what to tell her.

ALBERTINE AT 40:
Don't worry. She'll choose for herself...All you can do is watch her go and have a good cry, 'cause you're going to feel responsible. It's always our fault. Always!

ALBERTINE AT 30:
Before you know it she'll be a woman, cooped up like the rest of us. Or cast out like the lepers...Did it ever strike you, Madeleine, with all your brains, that those are our only choices?

MADELEINE:
Would you be any happier if you'd made the other one?

ALBERTINE AT 30:
That's not the point. If I were younger, I'd look for a third choice...   *Silence.*   That's what I'll tell Thérèse...If I can ever talk to her....

MADELEINE:
No harm trying.

ALBERTINE AT 40:
I did try.   *to ALBERTINE AT 50*   You did the right thing.

ALBERTINE AT 30:   *to MADELEINE*
What do you think of that?

MADELEINE:
If my daughter does what I've done, I don't think she'll be wrong.

ALBERTINE AT 70:
Poor Madeleine. But maybe you wre right. Maybe there's more than one truth. Sometimes what's true for us doesn't hold for someone else. You were happy the way you were, Madeleine. When you come right down to it, I was probably jealous....

ALBERTINE AT 30:
I'm not jealous of her!

ALBERTINE AT 40:
Me neither!

ALBERTINE AT 70:
    You just never admitted it...

ALBERTINE AT 50:
    At times...I don't mean I'm jealous exactly, no, no, I
    like my independence too much...But when she comes to
    see me at the restaurant, with her little
    granddaughter, all dressed up, I think maybe I'd have
    liked that too, grandchildren to play with, and spoil...

ALBERTINE AT 70:
    Mind you, if I hadn't married a buffoon, I might have
    felt differently.

ALBERTINE AT 40:
    Oh, come off it! She's right, men are all the same, they
    get us every time. They're in control, what do you
    expect? As long as we let them, they take advantage.
    'Cause they're not idiots. It's their world, they made it.
    Thérèse got a taste of that, you know. Prince Charming
    on a fake charger with a rented costume! Believe it or
    not, she came home one day with a guy who looked
    normal. Like a jerk, I figured leave well enough alone,
    he's better than what she usually drags in! You can't
    imagine the winners I've seen, things the lowest whore
    wouldn't touch! Anyway...he was good looking, he was
    nice, he had gentle eyes. Halleluia! But when I asked
    him what he did for a living and he told me he was a
    bus driver, I figured this is too good...something's
    fishy...And wouldn't you know it, he told me he'd
    known Thérèse for a long time. Ten years ago he was
    an attendant at parc Lafontaine...

    ALBERTINE AT 30 starts.

Oh yes...It all fit, he was about ten years older than
her, it all made sense...It took him ten years to get her,
and he got her. And Thérèse knows the score. She's not
eleven any more, she's twenty, she knows what she's
doing. And she knows what he wanted to do to her. But

here's what infuriates me...she's decided she's going to marry him! 'Cause he's handsome. 'Cause other women are jealous. 'Cause it pisses me off! And you wonder why I want to kill! My own daughter's going to marry a man who almost raped her ten years ago...who could start again at any time with anybody. That's it, that's men in a nutshell: they find a hole, they stick it in!

Long embarrassed silence.

ALBERTINE AT 40:
Forgive me. You especially, Madeleine. What you don't know won't hurt you, but I'll bet your Alex isn't perfect. It's not possible. He's got to be hiding something.

ALBERTINE AT 70:
He's not expected to be perfect. Watch out...you're making judgements...

ALBERTINE AT 60:
And I suppose you don't? You won't look at me, won't speak to me...you act like I don't exist!

ALBERTINE AT 70:
I'm not perfect either...

ALBERTINE AT 40:
Anyway, her Alex...I never trusted him.

ALBERTINE AT 50:
That's not true...In fact you had your eye on him once...

ALBERTINE AT 40:
That twerp? Come off it!

ALBERTINE AT 70:
But it's true. I remember. He was a twerp, but that was his charm...You could tell he wasn't dangerous...But Madeleine was too fast for me...

MADELEINE:
Stop talking about me like I'm not here! And don't talk about Alex that way, it's embarrassing...

ALBERTINE AT 50:
No one will steal your prince...

ALBERTINE AT 40:
God, no!

MADELEINE:
If you don't want to believe me, don't...I'm sure you have your reasons for hating men...   *She smiles.*
I don't...Maybe I'm content with very little, maybe my happiness is trite and insignificant,
but...   *Silence.*   It's funny...I don't care. I think . . . I think I'd rather be happy in my own modest way than spend my life living some grand tragedy.   *Silence.*   When those two beams of light come round the bend, you can all rest assured, I'll be happy, perfectly happy...and that's all I have to say.

ALBERTINE AT 70   *softly*
You've been gone so long, Madeleine, I have trouble seeing you clearly. I remember you well but the image is blurred...I know you were a good person...the best in the family. Mind you, Gabriel and Edouard were okay, but they were men...You were always so patient...

MADELEINE:
You talk about me in the past. That means I'm not here, doesn't it?

ALBERTINE AT 70:
Yes. You've been gone...oh...I was still working at parc Lafontaine...That's a good twenty years...

MADELEINE:
I won't have lived long...Was I happy til the end?

ALBERTINE AT 70:
Come over here and sit beside me...

MADELEINE sits at her sister's feet.

I thought your hair was redder.

MADELEINE:
Red?

ALBERTINE AT 70:
As I recall, your hair was red that summer...

MADELEINE:
It was the sun...

ALBERTINE AT 30:
If I spent three years in the sun, my hair would still be black.

ALBERTINE AT 70:
When you left us, I lost my only confidante...The phone didn't ring any more...Ah! For a long time we didn't talk much 'cause you were mad when I turned my back on the kids...though deep down, I think you understood...but we started phoning again, at first just to keep in touch, then 'cause we really needed to see each other...and when you brought your granddaughter to see me for the first time, and I saw how fat you'd gotten...I laughed so hard! Mind you, maybe that's why I have trouble remembering you...The last few times I saw you, you were so fat...

MADELEINE:
Don't exaggerate!

ALBERTINE AT 70:
Well...

ALBERTINE AT 50:
> We didn't recognize each other. I missed you so much!

> *Silence.*

MADELEINE:
> Bartine...Did I suffer much before I died?

ALBERTINE AT 70:   *after hesitating*
> Yes...Don't go...stay with me a bit...The night will be long...

MADELEINE:
> You're right, it does smell funny here...

ALBERTINE AT 70:
> You see, I don't notice it any more...I've already forgotten...

ALBERTINE AT 30:
> It's getting chilly, eh?

MADELEINE:
> You're not used to it. It's August, summer's nearly over. But wait and see how well you'll sleep!

ALBERTINE AT 70:
> I hope so...

MADELEINE:
> You want a sweater?

ALBERTINE AT 30:
> No, no...

ALBERTINE AT 40:
> Hasn't been so cold this early for a long time...Another rotten summer!

ALBERTINE AT 30:
   I want to wait for your Prince Charming with his light
   beams.

   They smile at each other.

   I'd like to be far away from the house right
   now...Maybe on top of that mountain...From up there,
   the house must look tiny...Close your eyes, try to
   imagine that's where we are...Can you see it, way down
   below? A flicker of light, shining on the edge of
   night...It looks so peaceful from a distance. Two women
   on a verandah. I wonder what they're talking about.
   They look so happy. Both of them.

   Silence.

   Do you think they look happy?

MADELEINE:
   Yes.

ALBERTINE AT 30:
   Shall we visit them? Maybe they can tell us their
   secret...You know it already but I...

ALBERTINE AT 40:
   It's so dark. Why haven't they turned on the
   streetlights?

ALBERTINE AT 50:
   It's dark because the moon's not up yet. I like that. I
   feel protected.

ALBERTINE AT 30:
   Normally I'm scared of the dark, but here it's
   inviting...In the city I'm never aware the world exists,
   so vast...overwhelming.   *Silence.*   In the city, the
   world seems small.

ALBERTINE AT 40:
I suffocate in the dark...like the world's closing in on me.

ALBERTINE AT 30:
In the city, the world doesn't exist.

ALBERTINE AT 50:
When I was a kid, sometimes I'd imagine there was nothing beyond my school...My school was the world. A world with only kids. Little girls, skipping.

ALBERTINE AT 30:
Here goes...I'm going to cry. No. Not yet. God, that's what I need, a really good cry!

ALBERTINE AT 40:
I try sometimes. In bed. I go deep down inside myself, I tell myself you've got to cry, it'll do you good. But it's no use. I have no reason to cry, just to scream. When Thérèse shows up in the morning, bruised, drunk, trying to butter me up because she feels guilty, but still being a smart-ass 'cause it's the only way she can show her independence, how can I cry? I scream! She screams back, I scream louder, then mother joins in...If the three of us stood face to face, screaming our heads off, it would have precisely the same effect. We don't listen to what anyone's saying, we listen to ourselves scream! Thérèse is down at the French Casino on la rue Saint-Laurent surrounded by drunks, whores and drug addicts. That's her problem. I've raised two kids for nothing and I feel guilty because I know I did it badly. That's my problem. Mother had to leave her house at Duhamel to come and live in the city, and she's never got over it. That's her problem. Three brilliant generations!

ALBERTINE AT 70:
And instead of trying to understand, you do nothing but insult each other...

ALBERTINE AT 40 looks at her.

ALBERTINE AT 40:
I have enough problems, I don't need other people's!

ALBERTINE AT 70:
That's why you'll never get anywhere.

ALBERTINE AT 50:   *to ALBERTINE AT 40*
And you want us to believe you're intelligent!

ALBERTINE AT 40:
But I can't solve them. I've never set foot on la rue
Saint-Laurent, it terrifies me, and I've spent one week
of my life at Duhamel.

ALBERTINE AT 50:
That has nothing to do with it! Besides, they don't
expect you to solve their problems, they only ask you to
listen.

ALBERTINE AT 40:
They don't listen to me, why should I listen to them?

ALBERTINE AT 50 and 70 sigh in exasperation.

ALBERTINE AT 50:
There's no point trying to talk to you, is there?

*MADELEINE gets up and goes toward ALBERTINE
AT 50.*

MADELEINE:
How did you find out...I was gone?

ALBERTINE AT 50:
The telephone rang here one night. I had my coat on, I
was about to leave...

MADELEINE:
   It must have been a shock...

ALBERTINE AT 50:
   No...We'd been expecting it. You were sick for a long
   time, you know...

MADELEINE:
   I don't want to hear any more.

> She runs back to the Duhamel house, taking refuge with
> *ALBERTINE AT 30.*

ALBERTINE AT 50:
   I didn't go home. I went straight to your place to be
   with Alex...

ALBERTINE AT 30:
   Is that him? Look, I see headlights on the road...

MADELEINE:
   No, they're too big...must be a truck.

ALBERTINE AT 50:
   But...Alex was inconsolable.

ALBERTINE AT 40:
   All the while, Marcel creeps around, watching us...He
   doesn't cry when we fight, he laughs. A maddening,
   nervous laugh. In his crazy eyes there's this...pleading
   look...as if he were saying: "don't fight, it makes me
   laugh, I'm so frightened, you'll make me
   laugh!"   *Silence. She screams.*   If I'd strangled them
   both when I saw they weren't normal, I wouldn't be
   saddled with all this now!

ALBERTINE AT 60:
   More guilt...

ALBERTINE AT 40:
Sure, it was drilled into us, what do you expect?

ALBERTINE AT 70:   *to ALBERTINE AT 60*
What can you feel guilty about, you're drugged to the
eyeballs?

ALBERTINE AT 60:
So, you've finally noticed I'm here!

ALBERTINE AT 70:
How can I help it, you stick your nose in everything.

ALBERTINE AT 60:
Don't I have a right to speak? Are you ashamed?

ALBERTINE AT 70:
Yes.

ALBERTINE AT 60:
Mind you, you're probably right...So be ashamed, and
leave me alone...

ALBERTINE AT 70:
I asked you a question...

ALBERTINE AT 60:
Don't pretend you don't know the answer. You can't
have forgotten, I'm not that far behind you.

ALBERTINE AT 70:
I want to hear you say it out loud...

ALBERTINE AT 60:
Why, if you remember?

ALBERTINE AT 70:
To make sure...my memories are as terrible as I
think...so I can start selecting again...

ALBERTINE AT 60:

It's true, I've never told anyone...I kept it to myself...Look...my hands are shaking...my mouth's dry...but I can't take another yet, I have to wait half an hour...or it'll make me sick instead of better...Once...when the pain was unbearable...I took three...just to see...I ended up on the floor beside the bed...I was unconscious for hours...But if you only knew how good it feels...when I don't overdo it. They're wonderful, these things, you know. They...lighten you is how the doctor described it...I don't feel that knot in my throat, the weight on my heart...I can breathe freely...It vibrates around me, as if I can hear the motor of things...It's true...sometimes I lie on my bed and I listen to the motor of things...The world is a huge clock...everything has its purpose...

ALBERTINE AT 40:

Even you?

ALBERTINE AT 60:   *looking at ALBERTINE AT 50*

Mine is to pay for those who have no heart. I fooled myself for a while. I thought things would be okay...I went my own way, thinking the rest of the world wouldn't follow...but it did.

ALBERTINE AT 50:

No!

ALBERTINE AT 60:

Oh yes, it followed!

ALBERTINE AT 50:

I don't believe you!

ALBERTINE AT 60:

You can't afford to...Hang on to your illusions as long as you can...gain time, it's running out fast...

ALBERTINE AT 40:
What made you fall so low? What happened?

ALBERTINE AT 60:   *to ALBERTINE AT 70*
Now do you remember?

ALBERTINE AT 70:
Of course...I never forgot...

ALBERTINE AT 60:
One morning the police knocked on the door...I was
getting ready to go to work...I was singing...Right away
I knew something had happened to Thérèse. The two
cops sat down in the living room. I looked at their long
faces and I thought: Any minute now the world's going
to come crashing down on my shoulders. And the world
came crashing down on my shoulders...

> *Silence.*

very gently   They told me they'd found Thérèse in a
room on Saint-Laurent. They weren't sure if she'd died
of natural causes or if someone had...she was soaked in
her own blood...I had to go and identify the body, I
was the closest relative. The closest relative...I made her
for God's sake! And her husband, ha! He'd disappeared
long ago, I always knew he would. So, with the world
on my shoulders, I went to identify the body. When I
saw...her face swollen...the blood everywhere...the white
of her skin...

ALBERTINE AT 40:
Guilt...

ALBERTINE AT 60:
I asked myself, is this where my life was leading? Is this
the price I have to pay for a few years of peace? Is this
the outcome...here, today? Did I bring her to this...my
daughter...who I never knew how to manage? Or is it
just to punish me? And for what?   *to ALBERTINE
AT 50*   For you?

71

ALBERTINE AT 50:
   No! It's not true!

ALBERTINE AT 60:
   Tough! If you're so naive to think that your life depends
   on you alone, too bad for you. You want to believe you
   have a choice, that you can choose to be free, that you
   can end your days making bacon, lettuce and
   sandwiches with mayo for a bunch of customers who will
   thank you til the end of time? Fine! Go right ahead! Let
   me know how it feels when the world comes crashing
   down around you, when you find yourself alone with
   nothing but guilt staring you in the face. Because that's
   the way we've always been had, and still we don't learn!
   You know what? I should have danced on my
   daughter's grave, yes danced, because at least, at least
   she chose her own destiny!   *She covers her mouth.*

ALBERTINE AT 40:
   Is that why you started....

ALBERTINE AT 60:
   The pills? Let's say I was lucky to have an
   understanding doctor.

ALBERTINE AT 70:
   He told you not to overdo it...

ALBERTINE AT 60:
   I don't overdo it...

ALBERTINE AT 70:
   Not yet...

ALBERTINE AT 60:
   Sometimes I have no choice...It's that or insanity...I feel
   it coming...I can see Thérèse...Marcel too, who's drifted
   away for good...   *She stretches out her arms in a
   cross.*   The world...explodes! Rage comes back!

72

ALBERTINE AT 70:

> One day...or rather one night...the guilt will be too
> much...you'll take one too many...

ALBERTINE AT 60:

> Good! I'm glad! You never know, the door I open may
> lead to some place bearable. It can't be worse than here!

> *ALBERTINE AT 70 looks around her.*

ALBERTINE AT 70:

> Mind you, you're right, it's not as bad. They're going
> to revive you, deintoxicate you, put you into a new
> "home" as they say...They'll cure you of everything,
> except your memories...

MADELEINE:

> He's going to be late...That's what happens when he
> travels too far...I'm going in, it's cold...

ALBERTINE AT 30:

> I'll stay for a bit...

MADELEINE:

> You want a sweater?

ALBERTINE AT 30:

> Yes...Look, goosebumps...

MADELEINE:

> We'll talk tomorrow...

ALBERTINE AT 30:

> Yes, tomorrow...

MADELEINE: *looking out at the road*

> If he gets home before you go to bed, tell him not to
> make any noise. If I'm asleep he won't wake me...and if
> I'm awake, I'll let him know one way or another...

ALBERTINE AT 70:
    Madeleine...

MADELEINE:
    Yes...

ALBERTINE AT 70:
    Don't worry about it...getting old's not worth it...

    MADELEINE goes out.

    Silence.

    ALBERTINE AT 40 prepares to go into the house.
    ALBERTINE AT 50 wipes her counter top. With
    difficulty, ALBERTINE AT 60 opens her container of
    pills. ALBERTINE AT 70 sighs.

ALBERTINE AT 30:
    All alone in the middle of the world.

ALBERTINE AT 50:
    I'll do anything to keep that from happening! Anything!

ALBERTINE AT 60:
    Good luck...

ALBERTINE AT 40:
    If only Thérèse would come home...Please, don't let her
    do something crazy tonight...

ALBERTINE AT 70:
    Nothing will happen now...Mind you, that's just as
    well...an empty woman in front of an empty television
    in an empty room that doesn't smell good.   *Silence.*
    Is this what you call a full life?

    Silence.

74

ALBERTINE AT 50:
　Look...

ALBERTINE AT 40:
　What?

ALBERTINE AT 50:
　There she is...the moon.

The five ALBERTINES look at the sky.

ALBERTINE AT 60:
　I can't see it...Where did I put my glasses...　*She finds them and puts them on.*

ALBERTINE AT 70:
　It's beautiful...

ALBERTINE AT 40:
　Yes, beautiful...even from here.

ALBERTINE AT 30:
　It's so big.

ALBERTINE AT 60:
　...and red...

Silence.

ALBERTINE AT 50:
　You could almost reach out and touch it...

ALBERTINE AT 60:
　She's alone, too.

The five ALBERTINES slowly raise their arms toward the moon.

ALBERTINE AT 70:
　Touch it...maybe it's the same one...

ALL FIVE ALBERTINES: *as if they had made physical contact*
Ahhhhh…

The moon, solitary and blood red, rises.

Blackout.